Sports
Illustrated KIDS

I've Got the
No-Skateboard
Blues

by Anita Yasuda
Illustrated by Jorge Santillan

STONE ARCH BOOKS
a capstone imprint

VICTORY SCHOOL SUPERSTARS

Sports Illustrated KIDS *I've Got the No-Skateboard Blues*
is published by Stone Arch Books — A Capstone Imprint
1710 Roe Crest Drive
North Mankato, MN 56003
www.capstonepub.com

Art Director: Bob Lentz
Graphic Designer: Hilary Wacholz
Production Specialist: Michelle Biedscheid

Timeline photo credits: Shutterstock/Charles Knox (top
left); Sports Illustrated/John W. McDonough (bottom),
Lane Stewart (top right), Robert Beck (middle left & middle
12 right).

Library of Congress Cataloging-in-Publication Data
Yasuda, Anita.
  I've got the no-skateboard blues / by Anita Yasuda; illustrated by Jorge H.
Santillan.
    p. cm. — (Sports illustrated kids. Victory School superstars)
  Summary: Tyler Trofee would like to spend all his time doing skateboarding
tricks, but his parents are tired of his recklessness and are insisting that he pay
for all the things he has destroyed around the neighborhood—will he learn to
be more responsible in time to get a new skateboard for the big contest?
  ISBN 978-1-4342-2244-2 (library binding)
  ISBN 978-1-4342-3866-5 (pbk.)
  1. Skateboarding—Juvenile fiction. 2. Responsibility—Juvenile fiction. [1.
Skateboarding—Fiction. 2. Responsibility—Fiction.] I. Santillan, Jorge, ill. II.
Title. III. Title: I have got the no-skateboard blues. IV. Series: Sports Illustrated
kids. Victory School superstars.
  PZ7.Y2124Iv 2012
  813.6—dc23   2011032820

TYLER TROFEE

Skateboarding

AGE: 10
GRADE: 4
SUPER SPORTS ABILITY: Super shooting in basketball

 VICTORY SCHOOL SUPERSTARS

 CARMEN

 DANNY

 ALICIA

 KENZIE

 JOSH

TABLE OF CONTENTS

T & T
Skatepark

VICTORY SCHOOL MAP

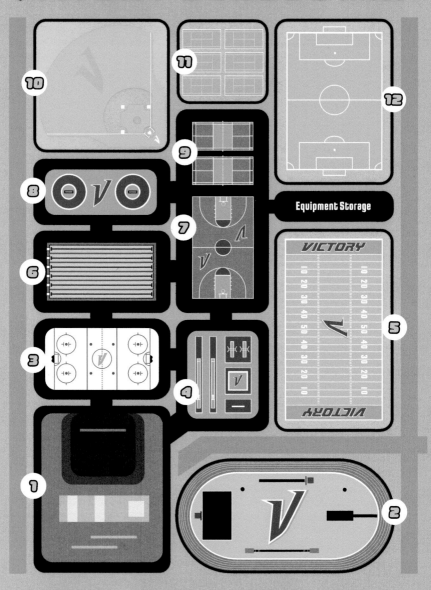

1. BMX/Skateboarding
2. Track and Field
3. Hockey/Figure Skating
4. Gymnastics
5. Football
6. Swimming
7. Basketball
8. Wrestling
9. Volleyball
10. Baseball/Softball
11. Tennis
12. Soccer

When I'm not busy with basketball, I love to skateboard. There isn't a curb I haven't jumped or a rail I haven't ridden in this town.

"It's awesome!" says my friend Josh, checking out the ramps and other obstacles. Josh goes to Victory, too. He has perfect footwork on the ice. He never loses his balance on a skateboard either.

"Wait until you ride here," I say. "This park is *fast*! Watch this."

I drop in on the ramp, zoom over, and launch into the air. I grab the bottom of my board to soar over the clothesline.

Ahhh! The back wheels snag on it. My arms go up. My legs feel like they are about to go down. I'm ready to fall at any second.

"Woooooooh!" I shout.

I recover and break free. Snapping the tail of my board, I ollie onto my mom's favorite bench. It breaks in two with a *craaaaack!* I guess she needs a new one.

Next is my special move, the skate and dunk. I grab my basketball and skate hard toward the hoop.

I leap up from the board and dunk the ball. My skateboard does not rebound off the garage door like I planned. I'm left dangling from the rim when my board flies into the street.

"Tyler," yells Josh, "the garbage truck is coming!"

"Noooooo!" I shout.

I watch helplessly as my skateboard meets with twenty-five tons of stinky doom. *Cruuuunch!*

Mom and Dad come running from the house to see what happened. When Mom sees the damage, she freezes. "Tyler, my bench!" she yells.

"On the bright side," I say, "we have two chairs now."

Dad looks at the bent basketball hoop. "Tyler, what do you think you were doing?" he asks.

"Creating the best skatepark ever," I say.

Mom and Dad exchange looks. Josh must know I'm about to get a lecture. "See you later, Tyler," he says, quickly skating away.

"Where is your responsibility? You haven't done your homework or helped around the house for weeks," says Mom. "And then there's your bedroom. Not only is your floor covered with stuff, but there is a pizza box on your bed!"

"I meant to do those things, honest," I say. "I just got busy."

"Being busy is not an excuse," Mom went on. "Your father and I expect you to be responsible and to care for your sports equipment." As Mom speaks, her eyebrows nearly touch. Oh boy, this only happens when she is really mad.

"That skateboard was new," says Dad.

"Another hoop ruined," says Mom, shaking her head. "And my bench!"

"I'll fix them all," I tell my parents. "Follow me." I lead them into the garage and hold up a tube of super glue.

"Super glue doesn't repair everything," says Mom, "and it certainly doesn't help with homework or chores."

"You will have to replace everything you broke," says Dad.

"I'll do odd jobs in the neighborhood," I say. "You'll see. I'll pay you back in no time."

"I know you think we are being tough," says Dad, "but this will be good for you."

"You will learn about responsibility," adds Mom.

Right now, I'm not worried about some lesson. I just need to get busy earning cash.

CHAPTER 2

Huge News!

"You missed one," says a voice behind me.

"Yes, Mrs. Marshall," I reply, digging deeper into the dirt.

Mrs. Marshall, my neighbor, has weeds. Those weeds are now my problem, since she is paying me to get rid of them. I'll waste the whole morning weeding that garden. This is so unfair!

"And don't forget to water my flowers," she adds.

"Yes, ma'am," I mutter through clenched teeth. I had been at it for an hour, and now the sun was overhead. This was not fun.

I turn on the water hose. A familiar sound reaches my ears. *RUMMMMBLE.*

It's Josh skating up the street. I sure am happy to see him. Josh rides alongside to the curb. He pulls off a smooth kickflip. *Sweet!*

"Look," he calls, waving a piece of paper.

"Unless that is a get-out-of-jail-early card," I say, "it's not going to improve my day."

"Want to bet?" asks Josh with a grin.

I grab the flyer he's holding out.

"No way!" I cry. "A skatepark just opened in town!"

Josh nods. "It's the biggest one yet," he says. "I am so tired of jumping curbs. There must be lots of ramps and rails."

"And a huge bowl," I add, my eyes glued to the paper. "It'll be the coolest place around."

"Hurry up!" says Josh. "We don't want to be the last ones there."

"Well, I'm not exactly done," I say, looking at the weeds and the lawn.

Josh shrugs. "Your choice, dude," he says, turning to leave.

"Hey wait!" I call after him.
"Mrs. Marshall just left for the store. I guess no one will miss me for a while."

"Yeah," agrees Josh, "she'll probably be gone for hours."

"Skatepark, here I come!" I cry, flinging down the hose. As I hurry after Josh, I can feel myself flying down the halfpipe.

Grounded

The lot near school isn't empty anymore. It is a concrete wonderland of ramps, bowls, and banked turns.

There are dozens of skaters shredding. I spot my friend Alicia taking a break by the water fountain.

"Hey, Alicia, can I borrow your board for a few runs?" I ask.

"Nothing crazy, Tyler," instructs Alicia. "I don't want it cracked."

I draw a halo above my head, and Alicia hands over her board.

"Look out!" I yell. I race up the ramp at an angle. The board's trucks lock on the edge. I grind along it. Then lift up the nose and turn away back down.

"This park is so much fun!" I say to Josh, taking a pause in my run.

"Yep, and next month is the official opening," he replies. "There's a best trick contest." Josh points to a large poster.

"We have to be in it," I say.

I am about to ride up the ramp, when I hear a sharp voice. "Tyler!" It's Dad. He doesn't look happy. The vein in his forehead is going 3-D. "Get in the car!" he yells.

"Thanks, Alicia," I say, giving her back the skateboard.

Dad starts into me as soon as I am in the car. "Do you know how irresponsible it was to leave Mrs. Marshall's before you were finished?" asks Dad.

"I was coming right back," I fib.

"You left the hose on her flower bed," says Dad.

Gulp.

We pull onto our street. A brown river flows toward the car. There are flowers everywhere. Mrs. Marshall's gnome is swimming.

"Well, at least the weeds are gone," I say.

"You are grounded," says Dad, "until you can show that you are responsible."

My head hurts. Things couldn't be worse. There is finally a skateboard park in town, and I am not allowed to go! I have to make things right. But how can I do that?

4

Riding on Chickens

For the next thirty days, my neighbors keep me busy. I weed, cut grass, and replant Mrs. Marshall's flower beds. She forgave me after I bought her a new gnome.

Even my parents are pleased. "Good work this month, Tyler," Dad says. "I know how much you've missed skateboarding. I think you deserve a few hours at the park."

"Thanks, Dad!" I say. Giving him a smile, I take off.

When I get to the park, I have another problem. I don't have a skateboard or even the money to rent one. Then I spy Marty, the skatepark manager, pitching a can into a trash bin. I have an idea.

"Hey, Marty," I say. "Could I earn a skateboard rental?"

Marty grins. "What do you have in mind?" he says.

"Well, I could pick up trash," I suggest.

"Sounds good," says Marty, handing me a garbage bag. "One bag of trash equals one rental."

"You have a deal," I tell him, slinging the garbage bag over my shoulder.

While picking up soda cans, I imagine myself on center court. *Tyler Trofee rushes to the hoop. He flies through the air. Quickly he wraps the ball between his legs and slams it.*

The can sails into recycling. I raise my arms pretending that Victory has won the state championship.

"Hey, Tyler," says Marty, waking me from my daydream. "How about taking those boards down to the curb for me?"

I follow his gaze. Wow! It is a huge pile of broken decks. Some are missing their noses. Others are broken in two.

"Can I have some of those?" I ask.

"Sure," says Marty, "but you know they can't be fixed right?"

"I know," I say. "I have a plan." The boards are step two in making things right at home again.

Soon enough my work is done, and I am back at the rental desk.

"Here you go," says Marty. He hands me a board that is covered in chickens. I think they are dancing. One is playing the flute. At least I have my own helmet. This is going to be embarrassing.

"Chickens . . . seriously? Chickens?" I ask. "This is what I get after all my work?"

"Take it or leave it," says Marty. "But it's the only board I have left to rent."

"I guess there are worse things," I say. I head out to the park. I can't wait to ride — even if it *is* a chicken board.

Josh gives me a nudge when he sees me. "Nice board," he says, snorting back his laughter.

"Just wait and see what these chickens can do," I reply.

I peer over the edge of the halfpipe. The front wheels touch the ramp. *Yes!* I travel to the other side and grab the lip. I push my body straight into the air. My free hand holds the board. When I let go, my landing is anything but smooth. Down I come. *Thump!*

I hear a chorus of *cluck clucks*. I shrug them off. All I have to do to get better is practice. There is no time to wait. I am up at the top of the ramp again. I am going to nail this handplant in time for the contest.

Contest Day

The morning of the contest arrives. After breakfast, my parents and I go to the skate shop. I know just which board to choose. One with no chickens!

"Seventy-eight, seventy-nine," I say counting out my money on the counter. Uh-oh, do I have enough?

"Tyler," says Dad putting his hand on my shoulder. "You've shown us that you can be responsible."

"We'll help you buy your board," adds Mom, smiling.

"Wow! Thanks," I say.

We hop back in the car. "Let's go," I tell my parents. "We can't be late."

The skatepark is packed. There are free hot dogs and plenty of tricked-out skateboards. Even people who have never ridden before get to try it out.

Opening ceremonies are about to begin. Principal Armstrong is on hand to cut the ribbon. "Skateboarding is about having fun," says Principal Armstrong. "I want to see kids come here to enjoy themselves."

Next up is Eagle Sato and his team of professional skaters. They do tricks like spins, big aerials, and 360 flips. It is awesome. No one does it better than Eagle. Eagle balances on one hand. He grips his board with the other to do a handplant.

Now it is the kids turn to skate with the pros. We all want to show off our best tricks. "Come on, Josh," I say, grabbing my new board.

Josh does spin after spin. Alicia carves up the bowl. Some of the other Victory kids get some serious air off the mega ramp.

All I want to do is land my trick. I drop in. It's a perfect handplant. I lower down to the ramp and ride back down. This feels great. It feels even better that I earned the board beneath my feet.

But the best thing about the day is giving Mom her present back home.

"What is it Tyler?" she asks as I lead her into the backyard.

"I am sorry about breaking your bench," I say. "Maybe this will make up for it." I whip off the sheet. Underneath is a new bench. I made it from the broken skateboard decks.

"It's great," says Mom, giving me a hug.

"Mom, wait!" I yell as she sits down. "The super glue hasn't dried yet."

"Tylerrrrrrrrrr!"

My skatepark is finished. I drop the
paint brush and admire my sign. It reads,
"The T & T Skatepark Wants You!"

The Ts are short for Tyler Trofee. I'm a
student at Victory School for Super Athletes.
All the kids there have amazing abilities.
I never miss a shot in basketball, no matter
what!

GLOSSARY

halfpipe (HAF-pipe)—a U-shaped ramp of any size, usually with a flat section in the middle

handplant (HAND-plant)—a move in which the board is held to the feet with one hand while the skateboarder performs a handstand on a ramp or obstacle with the other

manager (MAN-uh-jur)—someone in charge of a business or a group of people

obstacles (OB-stuh-kuhls)—in skateboarding, objects that skaters can ride and perform tricks on

ollie (AH-lee)—a trick in which the skater kicks the tail of the board down and then jumps to pop the board into the air

responsibility (ri-spon-suh-BIL-uh-tee)—the quality of being trustworthy or dependable

SKATEBOARDING IN HISTORY

1958 The first skateboards are made by California surfers.

1963 The first national skateboarding competition is held.

1972 Polyurethane wheels are invented. They make skateboarding smoother and more stable.

1976 The first outdoor skatepark opens.

1978 The ollie, a skateboard trick, is invented.

1984 Vert skateboarding in empty swimming pools begins.

1990 The first All Girls Skate Jam is held.

1995 The first X Games are held. Skateboarding is a featured sport.

1999 The first Tony Hawk video game is released, making the sport even more popular.

2003 Skaters celebrate the first Go Skateboarding Day on June 21. This international event takes place annually.

2010 Professional skateboarder Rob Dyrdek starts Street League Skateboarding, a series of contests featuring leading street skateboarders.

Tyler Trofee Takes Home the Gold!

If you liked reading Tyler's skateboarding adventure, check out his other sports stories.

Nobody Wants to Play with a Ball Hog

In basketball, Tyler is a perfect shot. Since he can't miss, he quits passing to his teammates. The other boys are sick of how Tyler plays. When will he learn that nobody wants to play with a ball hog?

There's No Crying in Baseball

The Victory School students have challenged their teachers to a game of baseball. No one is more excited than Tyler. But when he sprains his ankle, he doesn't even want to go to the game. Maybe he forgot that there's no crying in baseball.

Beach Volleyball Is No Joke

Tyler loves a good practical joke, but his beach volleyball teammates have had enough. He has spent so much time on his gags, that he hasn't learned anything about the game.